SO-AZU-120

A Fairyland Costume Ball

Chloe
the Topaz Fairy

Amy
the Amethyst Fairy

The Jewel Fairies

Scarlett
the Garnet Fairy

India
the Moonstone
Fairy

Sophie
the Sapphire
Fairy

Lucy
the Diamond Fairy

Emily
the Emerald Fairy

ISBN 978-0-545-43389-1

10 9 8 7 6 5   14 15 16 17/0

Printed in the U.S.A.   40
This edition first printing, May 2012

A Fairyland Costume Ball

by Daisy
Meadows

SCHOLASTIC INC.

Red leaves drop from the trees.
It is fall in Fairyland.

Halloween will be here soon.
The Jewel Fairies are excited.

Halloween is a magical time in Fairyland. The fairy king and queen always throw a grand costume ball.

All the fairies dress up, dance, and celebrate. The Jewel Fairies want their costumes to be extra special.

Flora the Dress-up Fairy and Trixie the Halloween Fairy arrive at the Jewel Fairies' cottage.

They want to help their friends get ready for the ball.

Flora swirls her wand, and all kinds of costumes appear.

"Halloween is fun because you can dress up however you want!" says Trixie.

"Let's all look for costumes that match the color of our jewels," Sophie suggests.
"What a colorful idea!" Chloe agrees.

Amy searches through racks of dresses and stacks of masks, but she doesn't find anything special.

"What's wrong, Amy?" asks Trixie.
"I can't find the right costume for the ball,"
she explains.

"Do you want to look fancy? Silly? Scary?"
Trixie asks.

"I don't know," Amy admits. "I want to
surprise everyone."

"Hmmm." Trixie sighs. "We'll think of
something."

Finally, it's Halloween night.
The Jewel Fairies chat and laugh as they
get ready.

Scarlett puts on her tiara.
Sophie paints whiskers on Chloe.

Lucy puts on a snowy headband.
"You look delicious!" India tells Emily.

Amy is in the corner with Trixie.
"What are you up to?" Chloe asks.

"Trixie is helping me put the last touches on my costume," Amy says with a sly smile.
"What costume?" asks Scarlett.
"You'll see," Amy replies.

Finally, it is time to leave.

"Has anyone seen Amy?" India asks.

"It's like she disappeared," Emily says.

"She told me that she will meet you at the ball," Trixie explains.

With hats and crowns and masks and makeup, the fairies set out for the costume ball.

"Let's take a shortcut through the Enchanted Forest," says Sophie. "It's faster."

"And spookier," Scarlett adds.

The shadows are long and dark in the forest.
A low moan echoes through the trees.

Scarlett shivers. "What was that?" she asks.
"I'm sure it was just the wind," Emily says,
but her voice trembles.

The fairies look around.
They don't see anyone.
They hear the low moan again.

OOOOOOO, OOOOOOOOOOO

"It sounds like a ghost!" Lucy cries. She
grabs India's hand.

The fairies feel a chill as the air rushes around them.

"I'm worried about Amy," Sophie says. "She will be walking all alone."

At last, the Jewel Fairies reach the
Fairyland Palace.
It twinkles in the moonlight.
"It looks beautiful!" says Chloe.

"Let's hurry," Lucy says. "The ball is about to begin."

When they enter the palace, Queen
Titania spots the Jewel Fairies.
"Welcome," she says. "But where is Amy?"

Just then, they hear the low moan again.

OOOOOOO, OOOOOOOOOO

A burst of purple sparkles appears.
"Boo! I'm a ghost!"

The Jewel Fairies shriek with surprise.

They know that voice.

It's Amy!

"You scared us!" Scarlett declares.

"You really didn't know it was me?" Amy asks.

"Not at all. That's a terrific costume," Flora tells Amy.

"I made it myself," Amy says, "with a little magic, of course!"

"Now we're all here! Let's have some Halloween fun," India says.

The Jewel Fairies join in the festivities.

Emily and Scarlett bob for apples.

Amy and Chloe eat pumpkin cupcakes.

All the fairies dance the Monster Mash.

At midnight, it's time for a special toast.
The Jewel Fairies raise their punch glasses.
"Happy Halloween!" announce the king
and queen.

Amy clinks her glass. "Here's to another
magical year filled with surprises!"